BELCHING HILL

Retold by
Morse Hamilton

Pictures by
Forest Rogers

Greenwillow Books, New York

AUTHOR'S NOTE

Belching Hill *is my version
of "The Old Woman Who Lost
Her Dumpling," one of the
many Japanese tales intro-
duced to the west around
the turn of the century by
the colorful Irish-American
writer Lafcadio Hearn.*

*Details of my retelling are
based on "The Old Woman
and the Rice Cakes" from* The
Maid of the North *by Ethel
Johnston Phelps. Copyright ©
1981 by Ethel Johnston Phelps.
Reprinted by permission of
Henry Holt and Co., Inc.*

*"Hanako," the pig's name, comes
from two Japanese words with
the same sound. "Hana" can mean
both flower and nose. The "-ko"
is a diminutive of endearment
commonly added to girls' names.
Thus "Hanako" might be rendered
in English as "Little Flower-snout."*

Watercolors, gouache, and colored pencils were used for the full-color art.
The text type is Veljovic Book. Text copyright © 1997 by Morse Hamilton.
Illustrations copyright © 1997 by Forest Rogers. All rights reserved. No part of this
book may be reproduced or utilized in any form or by any means, electronic or
mechanical, including photocopying, recording, or by any information storage and
retrieval system, without permission in writing from the Publisher, Greenwillow
Books, a division of William Morrow & Company, Inc., 1350 Avenue of the
Americas, New York, NY 10019. Printed in Singapore by Tien Wah Press.
First Edition 10 9 8 7 6 5 4 3 2 1

Library of Congress Cataloging-in-Publication Data
Hamilton, Morse.
Belching Hill / retold by Morse Hamilton ; pictures by Forest Rogers.
    p.   cm.
Summary: An old Japanese woman with a talent for making rice
dumplings uses her wits to escape from a cavern filled with ogres.
ISBN 0-688-14561-2   [1. Fairy tales.   2. Folklore—Japan.]
I. Rogers, Forest, ill.   II. Title.   PZ8.H175Be   1997   398.2—dc20
[E]   96-10415   CIP   AC

For Niki—M. H.

For Steve—F. R.

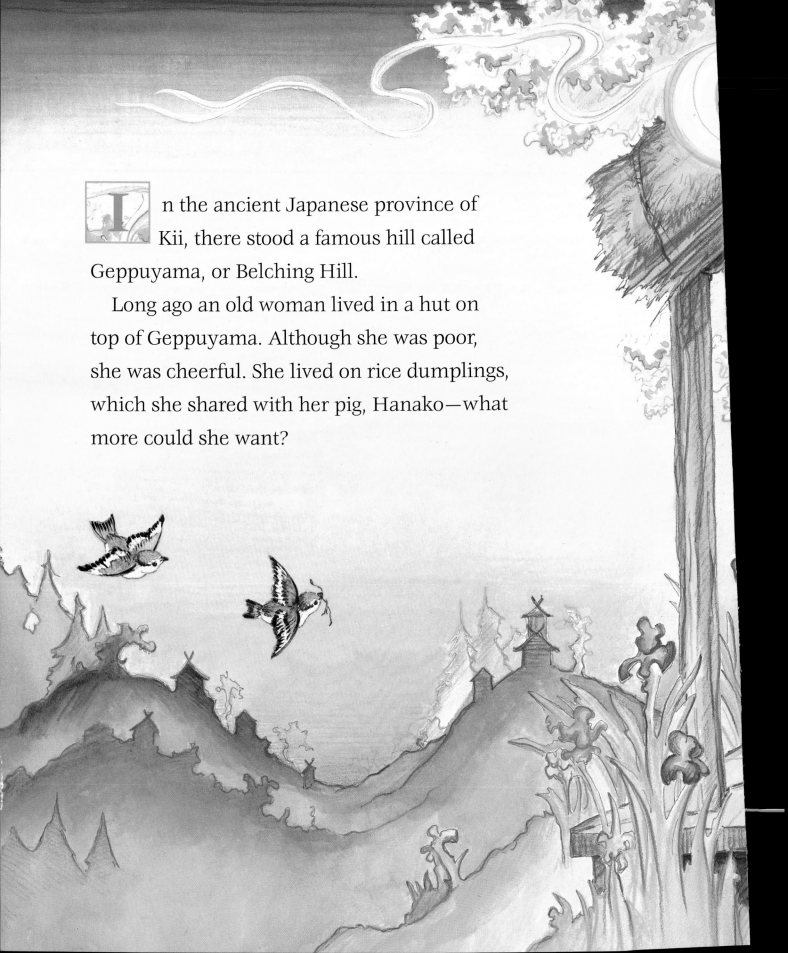

I n the ancient Japanese province of Kii, there stood a famous hill called Geppuyama, or Belching Hill.

Long ago an old woman lived in a hut on top of Geppuyama. Although she was poor, she was cheerful. She lived on rice dumplings, which she shared with her pig, Hanako—what more could she want?

One day the old woman picked up a dumpling when it was still piping hot, said "Atchie!" and quickly dropped it.

Being plump and slippery, it did not just lie there on the floor, but skittered out the door and rolled downhill.

Calling "Come back! Come back!" the old woman ran after it. It was all she had for her supper.

Ah, there it was, like a fat mushroom
in the grass. Just as the old woman bent
over to pick up her dumpling, a big
hand came out of a hole in the ground
and snatched it.

"Wait!" the old woman gasped.

But the hand withdrew into the hole.

Without stopping to reflect whether it was a wise thing to do, the old woman got down on her hands and knees, put her head in the hole, and crawled in. She was just in time to see the great, hulking shadow of a creature receding down an underground passageway.

"Stop!" she cried, hurrying after it. "Come back! That's *my* dumpling!"

The path sloped down to an underground river.
I must be inside my own hill, the old woman
thought, and for some reason the idea amused her.

At the river's edge the passageway opened up
into a great cavern. Along the wall, leaning against
each other for warmth, was a snarl of ogres—some
smaller creatures, too. It smelled like a bedroom
that had not been cleaned or aired in centuries.

As soon as the dumpling thief rushed in, all the other ogres fell upon him, growling and spitting, the way ogres do in every land. Fur began flying.

But that did not daunt the old woman. She walked right up to the thief, shook her fist in his hideous face, and said, wheezing (for she was out of breath), "What have you done with my dumpling?"

The ogre was noisily sucking his fingers. He looked away with all his eyes.

The other ogres crowded around.

"You cook the dumpling?" one of them asked the old woman.

"Yes, and it was a mean thing to do, to snatch it like that. That's taking something that doesn't belong to you. At least you could say, 'Thank you very much.'"

One of the ogres set a pot down before her and put a few grains of rice in her hand.

"Dump-lings, dump-lings!" the ogres chanted, licking their noses and snapping their teeth. "Cook dumplings—or, thank you very much, we will eat YOU!"

The old woman did not mind cooking—
in fact, it was what she liked to do best.
But how could she turn a few grains of
rice into enough dumplings to fill so
many stomachs?

Just then a small ogre handed her a wooden spoon. It was very old, very smooth, and decorated with ancient Japanese characters. As soon as she held it, she knew that it was a magic spoon. The old woman smiled. "Let's see what happens now," she said to herself.

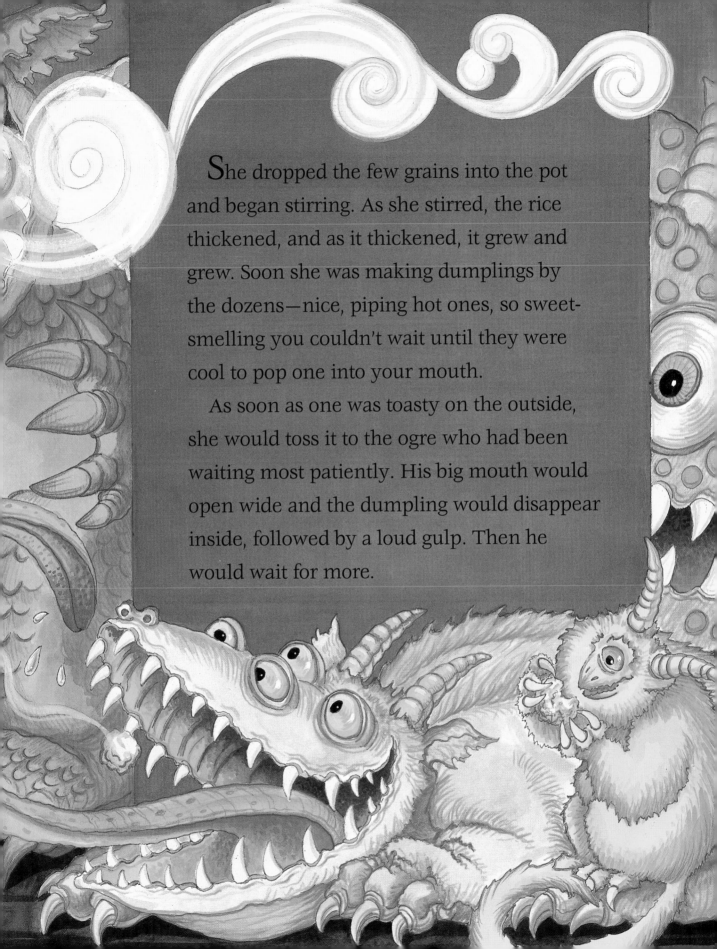

She dropped the few grains into the pot and began stirring. As she stirred, the rice thickened, and as it thickened, it grew and grew. Soon she was making dumplings by the dozens—nice, piping hot ones, so sweet-smelling you couldn't wait until they were cool to pop one into your mouth.

As soon as one was toasty on the outside, she would toss it to the ogre who had been waiting most patiently. His big mouth would open wide and the dumpling would disappear inside, followed by a loud gulp. Then he would wait for more.

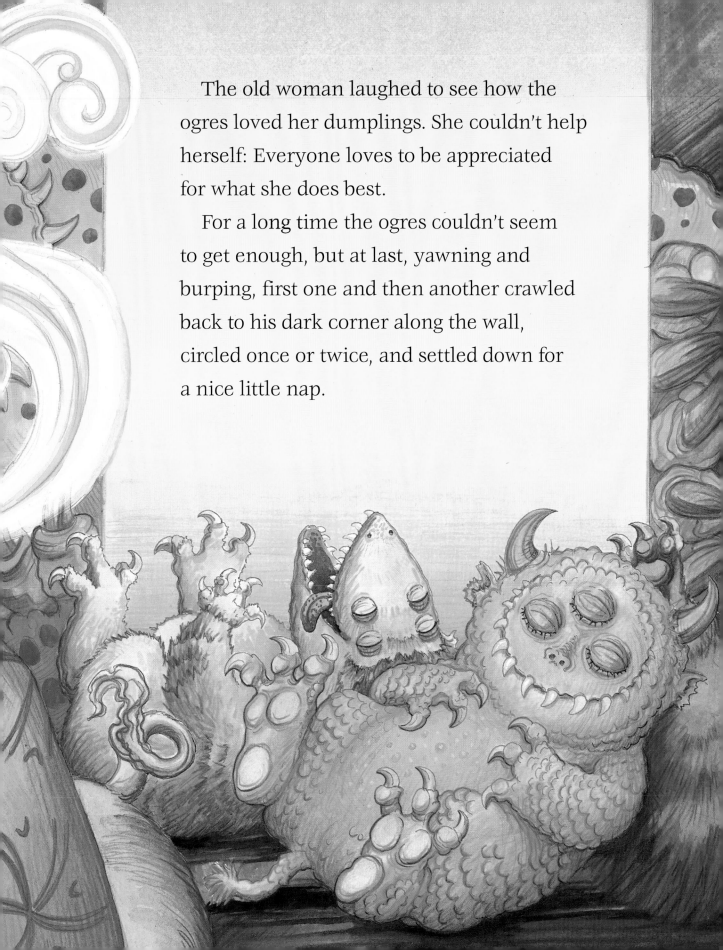

The old woman laughed to see how the ogres loved her dumplings. She couldn't help herself: Everyone loves to be appreciated for what she does best.

For a long time the ogres couldn't seem to get enough, but at last, yawning and burping, first one and then another crawled back to his dark corner along the wall, circled once or twice, and settled down for a nice little nap.

"Now I'll just go home, if you don't mind," the old woman said—very quietly, so that no one would hear over the loud snuffling and snorting. "And for my trouble," she added, chuckling to herself, "I'll just take this spoon and this pot with me, thank you very much. I think that's fair, don't you?"

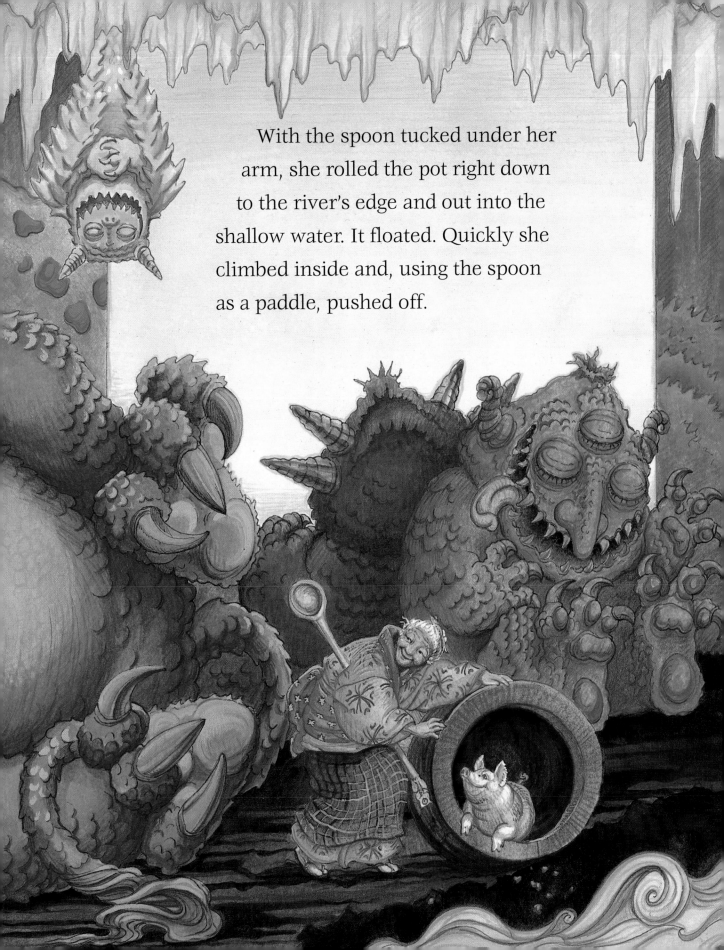

With the spoon tucked under her
arm, she rolled the pot right down
to the river's edge and out into the
shallow water. It floated. Quickly she
climbed inside and, using the spoon
as a paddle, pushed off.

Something woke the ogres. Maybe it was the old woman's gleeful laughter. First one eye opened, then another, then a third. Many eyes were watching her.

As soon as they realized what was happening—for ogres are notoriously dim-witted—they jumped up and ran to the river, waving their arms and shrieking.

"Come back! You have to cook the tasty dumplings! It's suppertime and we're starving!"

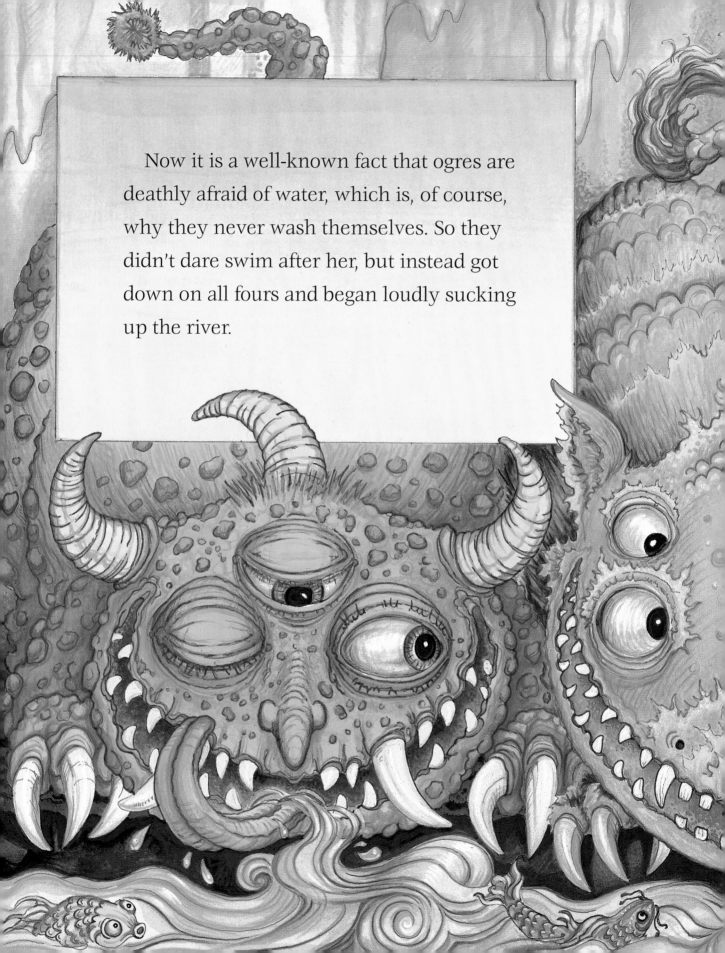

Now it is a well-known fact that ogres are deathly afraid of water, which is, of course, why they never wash themselves. So they didn't dare swim after her, but instead got down on all fours and began loudly sucking up the river.

The water level started to fall.
The old woman knew that when
the river ran dry, the ogres would
clamber across the stones to get
her. So the moment she felt the
pot touch bottom with a dull thump,
she called out, "Honorable Ogres,
I have something to show you."

Then she made all the animal faces she had learned as a child. First she was a fish and then a frog and then a pig. Finally she made her eyes bulge and her tongue hang out like an ogre.

That did it: The ogres couldn't keep from laughing. And, of course, as soon as they laughed, the river came spilling out of their mouths.

Soon the pot was up and spinning on the current, which swept it around a bend in the rocks and out into the light of day.

The old woman knew at once where she was. She steered to shore, climbed out, and began dragging the pot up her hill.

Farmers working in the rice paddies
nearby came to help her.

"Don't go yet," she told them when she was
safely home again.

Taking a few grains of rice from the jar she
kept by the window, she tossed them into the
pot. Soon the smell of piping hot dumplings
wafted from the hut. The farmers were in no
hurry to leave.

From then on, people came from far and wide to taste the old woman's famous dumplings. She was paid handsomely for doing what she loved to do.

Making dumplings scarcely seemed like
work to her. And if ever a dumpling fell
on the floor and rolled downhill, she called
out merrily, "That one is for you, dears!"

From deep inside the earth came the
rumble for which Geppuyama is justly
famous.